SARAH LEAN'S fascination with animals began
when she was aged eight and a stray cat walked
in the back door and decided to adopt her.
As a child she wanted to be a writer and used
to dictate stories to her mother, but it wasn't until
she bought a laptop of her own several years ago
that she decided to type them herself. She loves
her garden, art, calligraphy and spending time
outdoors. She lives in Dorset and shares the space
around her desk with her dogs, Harry and Coco.

www.sarahlean.co.uk

Also by Sarah Lean

The Tiger Days series in reading order:

The Secret Cat

The Midnight Foxes

The Riverbank Otter

Duckling Days

For older readers:

A Dog Called Homeless

A Horse for Angel

The Forever Whale

Jack Pepper

Hero

Harry and Hope

The Riverbank Otter

SARAH LEAN

Illustrations by Anna Currey

HarperCollins *Children's Books*

First published in Great Britain by HarperCollins *Children's Books* in 2018
HarperCollins *Children's Books* is a division of HarperCollins*Publishers* Ltd,
1 London Bridge Street, London, SE1 9GF

The HarperCollins website address is: www.harpercollins.co.uk

2

Text © Sarah Lean 2018
Illustrations © Anna Currey 2018

ISBN 978-00-0-816575-8

Sarah Lean asserts the moral right to be identified as the author of the work.
Anna Currey asserts the moral right to be identified as the illustrator of the work.

Printed and bound by CPI Group (UK) Ltd, Croydon, CR0 4YY

MIX
Paper from
responsible sources
FSC™ C007454

This book is produced from independently certified FSC™ paper
to ensure responsible forest management.

For more information visit: www.harpercollins.co.uk/green

To Peter Lean and Wells Rotary Club
for helping to bring stories to the children
of the Korup region in Cameroon.

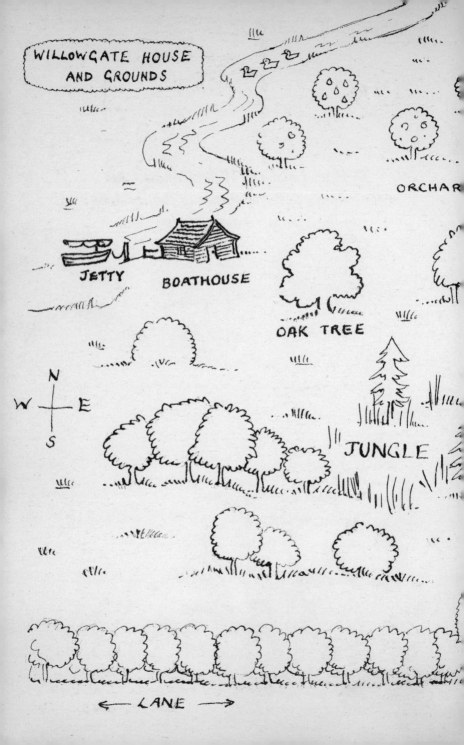

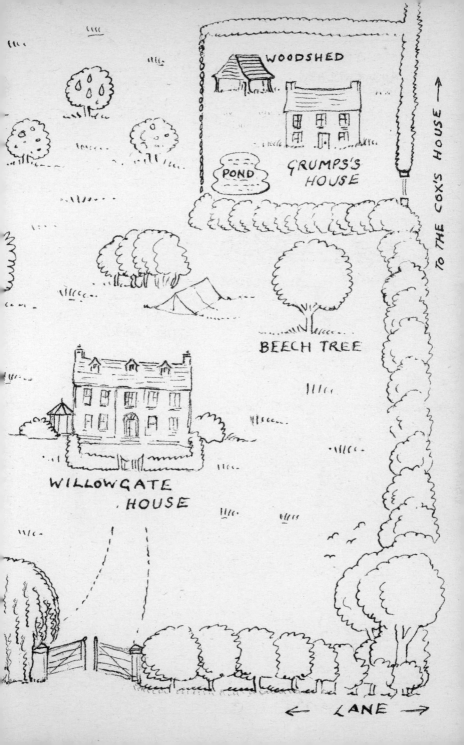

Chapter 1

Surprises

Tiger Days loved tigers. She lived in
a busy town and spent a lot of time
indoors where she liked to draw pictures of
tigers. But ever since Tiger had been visiting
her grandmother, May Days, at Willowgate
House in the countryside, she was beginning
to be more adventurous outdoors. May Days
used to live on a wildlife reserve in Africa,
and even now she sometimes looked after
animals that were in need of helping hands.

Tiger was on her way to Willowgate
with her dad. She never knew what might
happen during her stays and was often
nervous about new things. But she was
looking forward to sharing the summer
weeks with Holly the cat and her friend
Tom, who stayed with his grandfather
next door during the holidays too.

While driving along the country road,
all of a sudden Mr Days slammed on the
brakes.

"What happened?!" said Tiger, frowning.
Her tummy was now turning in a worried
twirl even before they had arrived.

Mr Days asked Tiger to stay put
while he got out of the car and walked

cautiously around to the front. "No need to panic, Tiger," he said. "Come and look."

Toddling across the road in front of the car was a duck with an emerald green head and orange beak and feet. It *could have* been unfortunate for the duck crossing the road at that moment.

"You are a very lucky duck," Tiger said and sighed with relief.

"Animals have no road sense," said Mr Days, hurrying the flapping, quacking duck to the verge on the other side. "Nobody teaches them to cross the road."

"They need to go to duck school," Tiger said, and laughed thinking about lessons for ducks: Feather Fluffing, How to Waddle Nicely, and How to Land on a Pond Without Doing an Embarrassing Roly-poly.

"Hopefully you won't have any more unexpected surprises at Willowgate," her dad said as they set off again.

Tiger wondered about this and felt

annoyed at herself for always feeling wobbly when something unexpected happened. Tiger decided that this visit would be different. She would stop feeling worried and instead be prepared for anything. Tiger made a plan…

"This time *I* am going to surprise May Days," she told her dad.

"How will you do that?" asked Mr Days.

"I'll think of something," said Tiger. She would have to wait for a good opportunity, but she was very determined she would surprise her grandmother for a change.

Willowgate House looked as raggedly
grand as ever, with its tall chimney pots
and the conservatory on the side that
leaned slightly to the left. Tiger asked
her dad to park the car at the end of the
drive, so they could go quietly up to the

house. The grass was even longer than the last time they visited and they had to lift their legs up high to get through.

"I am going to surprise May Days straight away," Tiger said.

Tiger crept around to the back of the house. May Days was in the kitchen putting biscuits on a plate. Holly the cat was sitting on a chair staring at the open back door, her eyes wide like green glass marbles, as if she already knew her favourite friend was about to arrive.

May Days saw Holly prick her ears, and turned round. "There's a tiger in the house!" she said, before Tiger could creep up on her.

Her first attempt at a surprise had not worked, but Tiger quickly decided she'd think of something bigger and better.

"You need a lawnmower, Mum," said Mr Days as he came in.

Tiger knew that her dad and May Days would spend the next few hours catching up over gallons of tea at the kitchen table before Mr Days drove home, so she quickly asked a few important questions first.

"Is the house still skewwhiff?" she said, hugging her grandmother while her dad waited for his turn. Willowgate House was very old and needed lots of repairs. They used the kitchen, but apart from that the house was not ready to live in.

"It is," said May Days.

"Will we still be sleeping in the tent in the garden?"

"Yes, we will."

"Are there any new animals to look after?"

"Not this time," May Days said. "And, before you ask, Tom's already here with Grumps next door and, yes, the foxes have gone."

Earlier in the year, Tiger and Tom had loved seeing the fox cubs who had made their home under the garden shed. Now the cubs were grown, they had left their den to find new homes.

Tiger put biscuits in her pocket, kissed her dad and said she'd see him in a couple of weeks.

"Well, this is a surprise," said Mr Days, who was used to Tiger clinging to him before he left. "Where are you going in such a hurry?"

Tiger grinned. It was easy to surprise her dad. "Tom and I have been waiting and waiting to make our own den in the shed," she said. "Come on, Holly."

The cat jumped down from the chair and
followed Tiger into the garden.

Tiger ran to the gap under the hedge
between Willowgate and Tom's
grandfather's house. Summer growth had
made the hedge thicker than ever and
Tiger had to scrabble through on her
elbows and tummy, although the tunnel
was about the right size for Holly.

Tiger could hear Tom and Grumps in the kitchen and she gently pushed Holly ahead through the open door.

"Hey, it's Holly!" said Tom.

Tiger jumped out from behind the door. "And me!" she said, pleased that she had made Tom jump when she sprang out.

"How is our little wildlife expert?" said Grumps. "Any animals at Willowgate to keep you busy this holiday?"

"Not today," said Tiger and she told them the news that the foxes had gone from under the shed.

"At last we can make our den!" said Tom.

They wanted to start right away and
together they scrambled back under the
hedge and raced across Willowgate's wild
garden, fighting their way through the
tangled grass, with Holly leaping closely
behind.

The shed was partly hidden by bushes
and trees, and the windows were covered
in dusty boards. Tiger and Tom had only
been in the shed briefly once before, so
they were excited to explore it properly.

They smiled at each other and pushed
on the large door that creaked as it
swung open. Sunlight peeped through
gaps between the planks of the walls.

An enormous green mound, as big

as a car, loomed in the middle of the
floor. When they had first seen it,
they'd convinced themselves it was a

monster, but now they knew it had to be something else…

"Maybe it's a big pile of logs like in Grumps's shed," said Tom, "or a car." He crouched to look underneath, but there was no sign of any wheels.

"It would be good if it was a giant lawnmower," said Tiger, thinking she could run back up to the house and tell her dad he could mow the long grass for May Days. Tiger hoped it wouldn't be a nasty surprise and was determined not to be worried, whatever it was. It was about time they found out.

Holding the corners of the green tarpaulin, Tiger and Tom tugged it away, blowing up a cloud of dust. They coughed and blinked, and their mouths fell open at what was underneath. There, left upside down many years before, was a wooden boat. Tiger bent over to read the upside-down name painted on the side.

Spinaway

Chapter 2

Spinaway

Tiger and Tom asked May Days and Grumps to come down to the shed so they could show them what they'd found.

The grandparents took down the boards from the windows to let in more light. Dust floated in the air as sunshine streamed in. They gathered around *Spinaway*, which was lying upside down off the floor on four long blocks of wood, while Holly sat on top of the boat.

"We didn't expect to find a ship in the shed," said Tom.

"Actually, this is not a ship. It's a twelve-foot sailing dinghy with a clinker-built wooden hull," said Grumps. "It's fine to call it a boat, though," he added.

Tiger and Tom stared at Grumps with their mouths open.

"How do you know all that?" asked Tom.

"I sailed as a boy," Grumps beamed. "And this is not a shed – it's a boathouse." He opened the big double doors at the other end and beckoned them over. Behind the boathouse, a concrete slope, called a slipway, led down to a wide river. As the garden was overgrown, with many parts still unexplored, the children hadn't even known there was a river there. The water glinted in the sunlight. But, of all the things they could have discovered, water was one of Tiger's least favourite. Despite her promise to herself, she began to worry.

Once, Tiger had been in a blow-up rowing boat with her dad at the seaside. She remembered how wobbly she'd felt bumping over the waves, and how she had panicked when the boat tipped up and she fell in. Even though she was wearing armbands and could swim and the water wasn't very deep, it wasn't a nice memory at all.

Tom had
already found blue
lifejackets in a box.
Grumps found
Spinaway's mast
and the sail, which
was rolled up in a
bag. A little sewing would fix the tear.

"I would be happy to restore *Spinaway*
to former glory, as she needs a little bit of
work before she would be fit for us to sail
in," Grumps said.

"I can't wait to be on the water," said
Tom, while Tiger tried very hard not to
feel anxious about what might lie ahead
this holiday.

May Days seemed very happy to let Grumps take care of the boat. "I have some clearing to be getting on with up at the house," she said. "Looks like there's some cleaning up to do here too!"

"Holly has already started dusting," said Tiger. The cat was nosing in a corner and had cobwebs on her whiskers. "I think I'll help her. I want to have a look around and think about what sort of den we can make," she said, hoping this would mean she wouldn't have to go out in the boat.

Now there was daylight coming into the boathouse, they could see there was a lot more to it than just a place to store *Spinaway*. There were wooden ladder-

steps beside the back double doors, and
Tiger clambered up to the loft-gallery
where she could just about stand up
under the sloping roof. She climbed over
piles of boxes, ignoring the wooden oars,
an anchor and coils of rope. Behind all
the sailing things she wasn't interested in
Tiger found a triangular window looking
out over the river. She rubbed the dust
from the glass with her sleeve to see out.

Drooping across the river on the other bank were willow trees, much smaller than the one at the end of Willowgate's drive. At the side of the slope, hidden behind lots of reeds, was a jetty – a small wooden pier you could walk on, out over the water to where a boat could float. On the post at the end of the pontoon was a duck. It looked exactly like the one Tiger had seen on the road. It flapped and flew

off, landing smoothly in the river. Tiger decided what she wanted the den to be for, and bounded down the steps to find Tom.

Before Tiger could say anything, Tom said, "I've got a brilliant idea. We could make the boathouse into a pirate den!"

Tiger wasn't expecting Tom to say that. Tom was excited about being a pirate, bravely roaming the river in the boat, and Tiger felt too embarrassed now to tell him that she was scared. She smiled at Tom and tried to look happy about being a pirate.

"That sounds great, but *my* idea is that we make it a nature spotter's den and learn about wildlife," she said, hoping she could persuade Tom to change his mind.

"But this is a perfect place to make a pirate den," said Tom, who had his own strong idea. "We can walk the plank on the pontoon and fly a skull and crossbones flag from the boat!"

"We could," said Tiger, "but we could also have a table and chairs and sit upstairs with binoculars and draw all the animals and wildlife we find."

Tom frowned a little. "We can pretend the river is the sea and go sailing to look for treasure," he said. "Grumps could teach us how to sail and I really, really want to learn!"

"But May Days could teach us about all the river animals," said Tiger, although it made her feel uncomfortable to think she would be spoiling things for Tom.

"This boathouse is so big," said Grumps, hearing the children's disagreement. "Lots of room for lots of ideas!"

Disappointed in herself and feeling awkward, Tiger looked at the floor. Tom looked at the ceiling. Usually they wanted to do the same project – like being animal trainers or pet detectives – but not this time. Surely it would be much more fun if they were doing something together, but they'd need to agree first. Tiger could see how much Tom wanted

to be a pirate. It didn't seem fair to make
him do something else.

"We can do our own thing instead, if you
want?" said Tiger, trying to look cheerful.

"Only if you want to," said Tom quietly.

They agreed it might be better this
holiday to try their own different things.

"I'll make a nature spotter's den
upstairs," said Tiger.

"I'll make a pirate den downstairs,"
said Tom.

Tom and Grumps washed and dusted
everything for the boat and screwed
hooks into the walls to hang it up neatly.
Grumps checked for holes and rot in the
boat and declared that *Spinaway* only

needed sanding and repainting.

Tom made pirate plans with Grumps, but Tiger didn't have anyone to share her ideas with as May Days was busy up at the house. She sat on the slipway with Holly. The cat stretched out in the sunshine and fell asleep, and Tiger watched and watched the river hoping to see the lucky duck again, but it had gone.

In the tent that night, Tiger and May Days got into their sleeping bags on the camp beds.

"You've been very quiet today," said May Days.

Tiger hadn't wanted to be worried about unexpected things this holiday. But all she had succeeded in doing was making herself feel upset by not saying how she really felt about sailing on the water.

"I wish we hadn't found a boat," she said.

May Days held her hand. "I'm rather glad you did. Tom and his grandfather seem rather taken with *Spinaway*."

Both Tom and Grumps *were* very happy they had found the boat, and Tiger felt mean wishing they hadn't.

"Is there something else on your mind?" said May Days softly. "You can tell me."

Tiger took a deep breath and told the truth. "I'm scared of going on the water," she whispered.

"We all have things we are afraid of," said May Days, and squeezed Tiger's hand across the camp beds. "Perhaps, for now, you could think about something *you'd* like to do? Something important to you?"

Tiger decided she would concentrate on making her own den special instead.

Chapter 3

Lucky Day

Tom and Grumps were down at
the boathouse, having a jolly time
together. Tiger did what she liked best and
drew a picture of a tiger and taped it to
the wall of her den, but she had no luck
spotting wildlife and had nothing to write
in her journal. Feeling lonely without
someone to share her project, she came
back up to the house to find a friend, and
scooped up Holly, carrying her around

under one arm. She followed May Days
in and out of the conservatory while her
grandmother was busy cleaning some
plant pots.

"What's going on down at the
boathouse?" said May Days.

"Tom and Grumps are telling each other pirate jokes," Tiger said. "What do pirates eat at parties? Jelly Roger and cust-har-hard." But she didn't laugh as she was now feeling jealous that Tom was having such a good time without her.

After lunch, Tiger sat in the kitchen with Holly on her lap trying to think of what else was important to her. Then she remembered her earlier promise to herself to surprise May Days. Normally she would ask Tom for ideas, but he was still at the boathouse with Grumps.

Tiger was trying to think of something

clever by herself when May Days said, "I think we ought to take Holly to the vet."

"Why? What's wrong with her?" said Tiger, holding Holly up to look at her. The cat was as bright-eyed and fluffy-tailed as ever.

"Nothing, I'm sure," said May Days. "But as she spends more time with us than anyone else, we ought to make sure she has regular check-ups."

May Days didn't have a car, but Grumps offered to give them a lift and drop them off. He and Tom needed to go shopping for sandpaper to rub down the old white paint on *Spinaway*'s hull. There was a DIY store just outside the village and they would pick Tiger and May Days up on the way back.

Miss Popescu, the vet, had met May Days several times since she'd moved to Willowgate House so knew May Days had lots of experience with animals.

"And who is this gorgeous ball of fluff?" said Miss Popescu, smiling warmly when Tiger put the cat on the table.

"This is Holly Days," said Tiger. "We look after her at Willowgate."

Holly didn't mind the vet at all and paraded along the table, waving her tail high in the air.

"How can you tell if Holly is not very well?" said Tiger, keen to learn.

"I'll show you," said Miss Popescu.

Tiger learned how to check that Holly's teeth were strong, her ears clean, her fur glossy and her eyes bright, and she was allowed to listen through the stethoscope to hear Holly's heart beating steadily. Holly already seemed to know she was healthy and didn't flinch at the injection she had to have to keep her healthy, while Tiger stroked her to help her stay calm.

"You are very good with animals," the vet said.

"I learned from May Days," said Tiger.

Miss Popescu looked very thoughtful. "I have been talking to May Days recently because I've had no luck finding a home for another animal," she said.

This was just the kind of important news that Tiger needed. But was it another cat? A rabbit? A guinea pig? For a moment she wondered if it might even be a tiger! Tom seemed to have had all the luck so far. Would this turn out to be Tiger's lucky day?

"Willowgate is a very nice home," said Tiger, feeling lively now. "It has loads of rooms and the garden is huge and Holly loves it there. It's the perfect home for any animal."

Miss Popescu twitched her lips from side to side as if she was still deciding.

"What sort of animal is it?" Tiger asked, ready to make plans.

"It's an otter," said the vet, and explained that a kind person had brought the otter to her when they had found it injured on the road about six months ago. Tiger thought about her idea for a duck school and thought that otters might need one too, to stay safe. Tiger wondered what otters might need to learn. The thought made her feel warm and fuzzy inside and she linked her arms through her grandmother's.

"Can the otter come home with

us?" said Tiger, looking at May Days
pleadingly.

"It's a *wild* otter," said the vet gently.
"He was quite young when he was found,
but now he's recovered and fully grown,
with the help of some experts. He's not a
pet, though, I'm afraid."

The otter wouldn't be at home in
anybody's house and needed to go back
to the wild. Tiger had got it all wrong
and her shoulders slumped.

"Would it be possible for Tiger to see
the otter?" asked May Days. Tiger gasped
at this, as she'd never seen an otter in real
life before.

In the garden area at the back of

the vet's were pens for injured wild animals, and Miss Popescu said they could have a little peek. Tiger stood on a short stepladder and looked through a letterbox-sized hole in a solid door. From a wooden box of straw, a soft brown face with a pale grey chin poked out. The otter had bright eyes and white twitching whiskers and Tiger adored it instantly.

"What sort of home does he need?" said Tiger.

"Now, that is an excellent question," said the vet, smiling. "First, we need to find a stretch of river."

"There's one at the bottom of May Days's garden!" said Tiger.

"We've only just discovered it," said May Days, quietly chuckling.

The vet was happy to hear this news, but needed to be sure of many things about the river and what else lived there before the otter could be safely released.

"What we really need is someone to do some nature spotting," she said. Tiger explained that this was exactly what she

had been planning to do! Miss Popescu
told Tiger what to look out for either in,
on or around the river, and Tiger carefully
made lists in her Nature Spotter's Journal
of insects, birds, fish, mammals, water
and the environment. If Tiger spotted
everything on the list, it would show that
the river was healthy and could make a
wonderful home for the otter.

Tiger was thrilled at having this
important project to do. It was a big

responsibility. There were a few things on the list she hadn't heard of, but May Days would be there to help her.

Grumps came to pick them up and Tiger was excited to tell Tom about the otter, even though he didn't look quite as pleased as she did. Tom was much happier to talk about the pirate flag he'd made for the boat and his plans to find treasure.

When they arrived back at Willowgate, they all went down to the boathouse.

All the doors were open. May Days helped Tiger make seats for her den from upturned wooden fruit boxes with cushions on top. They glued a big map of the area to one of the boards from the windows

and hung it on the wall. They washed
the triangle window and polished it
clear. Tiger found it easier and more fun
to get on with things with May Days
there too, and it helped having a proper
plan.

Meanwhile, Grumps and Tom rubbed
sandpaper along the lines of the wood
grain on the boat's hull. Their faces

were white, their clothes were white
and Grumps's hair was whiter than ever.
Paint dust rose in the warm air, with the
shush-shush, *shush-shush* of the sandpaper
and the lovely smell of wood. Although
Grumps was always the opposite of
grumpy, he had an extra sparkle in his
eyes while he worked on the boat.

Soon they all began to talk about what colour to paint *Spinaway*.

Tiger suggested orange and black, but it didn't seem quite right to paint a boat with stripes like a tiger.

"Just black would be more piratey," said Tom. The two of them had very different ideas again.

"What is your favourite colour, Grumps?" asked May Days, which made the children smile at each other as it was obvious that Grumps was the right person to choose.

Grumps painted *Spinaway*'s hull summer-sky blue, and the name on the side in white. He sewed the tear in the sail with nimble fingers.

Tiger's project was beginning to look very promising. So was Tom's. By tomorrow, *Spinaway* would be ready to set sail.

"Can I give the otter a name?" said Tiger, who was too excited to fall asleep that night.

"What name did you have in mind?" said May Days.

"Lucky, because he is making everything turn out better than expected."

Chapter 4

Holding On

All hands were needed to turn *Spinaway*. The boat wasn't very heavy, but it was tricky to handle the curved hump of the hull as they rolled it over.

"It reminds me of the time I lifted an elephant out of a swamp," said May Days.

"By yourself?" said Tiger, eyes wide in surprise that her grandmother was strong enough to do that.

"With a winch, a Land Rover and

lots of help," said May Days, chuckling. It made Tiger feel more determined today than ever to find an opportunity to do something as surprising as her grandmother.

After cleaning the inside of the boat and chasing out woodlice and spiders, *Spinaway* was ready to launch. They carried it down the slipway to the river's edge and put up the mast. Grumps climbed in and Tiger felt jittery in case it toppled over, but couldn't help cheering with Tom when it floated safely on the water. Using the oars, Grumps rowed to the edge of the pontoon and tied the bow rope to the post.

"All aboard, me hearties!" Grumps

called. Tom was ready to set sail –

wearing a lifejacket, black tricorn hat

and striped T-shirt. He wore a black

eyepatch, but it made him giddy only

seeing out of one eye, so he kept it flipped

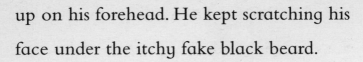

up on his forehead. He kept scratching his face under the itchy fake black beard.

"Anyone can tell you are a pirate even if you don't wear the beard," said Tiger.

"Good!" said Tom, taking it off. "Can I steer?" he said to Grumps.

"But it hasn't got a steering wheel," said Tiger.

Grumps pointed to a wooden stick called the tiller at the back of the boat, attached to the rudder under the water. Tom would have to push the tiller right to turn left, and left to turn right. "Steering is all back to front in a boat, but you'll soon learn," said Grumps.

May Days suddenly remembered she

had to go back up to the house as she was expecting a delivery and would have to miss them setting sail.

"Come on, Tiger. Aren't you getting in?" said Tom.

Tiger didn't want to go and was too embarrassed to tell Tom about being scared, especially after seeing him jump in the boat so bravely, even when it was rocking from side to side.

"I'd better wait here," said Tiger. "You might need someone to pull you back if it gets a leak," she said, so that Tom wouldn't guess she was afraid.

"You can be our health and safety checker because you think of all the things I forget to worry about," laughed Tom.

Tiger untied the rope from the post. Grumps pulled in the oars and hoisted the sail. The sail flapped as it rose and the breeze puffed it out like a plump pillow, surging forward and carrying the boat away.

Tiger felt proud of her friend, but within seconds something looked wrong. "Other way!" Tiger called from the pontoon

as Tom steered the boat into the trailing branches of a willow tree. "Other way!" she shouted again as Tom steered back towards the pontoon.

"I'm trying, I'm trying!" said Tom, not used to the tiller or the sails. "It's surprisingly tricky."

"Backwards!" squealed Tiger, as the boat headed towards her. The bow bumped into the pontoon post, knocking one of the oars into the river. *Spinaway* hadn't gone anywhere yet...

"We'd better stop a moment," Grumps said, as the oar bobbed in the water. "Tiger, would you tie the rope to the post again, please?"

"Good job I was still here," said Tiger.

Glad she was still on dry land, Tiger tied the rope as Grumps and Tom leaned out over the water to reach the oar. The knot Tiger made wasn't the right kind of knot. The rope unravelled and trailed towards the edge of the pontoon. Tiger grabbed the rope before it fell in the water, and pulled as hard as she could to save the boat from floating away.

Spinaway turned with the current and tugged Tiger along the pontoon. She held the rope above her head and went around the reeds to the slipway, hoping to pull the boat in to shore. *Spinaway*'s sail puffed out again with another gust of wind,

dragging Tiger into the edge of the river.
She was determined not to let go, afraid
what might happen to Tom and Grumps,
and leaned back as hard as she could.
Grumps finally caught the oar and pulled
it into the boat and saw what Tiger was
doing.

"Let go, Tiger!" he said quickly as Tiger
was now up to her knees in the water.
"Drop the sail, Tom!"

Grumps scrabbled to the bow and took
the rope from Tiger while Tom loosened a
rope and the sail collapsed down, stopping
the boat from spinning away.

"I thought I had to hold on," said Tiger.

"You are as strong as your grandmother,"

Grumps said. "But some things you hold on to and some things you have to let go." The current in the river was stronger than it looked and they all had to be careful. Tiger knew she and Tom were both lucky to have Grumps around to teach them what to do, but she felt uncomfortable about making mistakes. She decided instead to think about more important things. An unfortunate otter still needed a home!

The pirates had set off again and their voices faded down the river, when Tiger heard a buzzing sound coming from the front of the house. It sounded like an engine, but not a car. Louder and louder it buzzed as it came closer. May Days appeared, driving a sit-on lawnmower.

"What do you think of my delivery?" she called. She was obviously enjoying herself very much, and went backwards and forwards zipping through the long grass around the boathouse. "Oh! What happened? Your shoes are wet, Tiger."

Tiger sighed. She hadn't intended to surprise her grandmother with wet shoes. She would have to think of a better way of surprising her later. But she *had* found out something useful to tell May Days. "I'm checking the water like Miss Popescu asked."

"Jolly good," May Days said, waving as she zipped away. "I'll be in the garden, if you need me."

Tiger collected some water and lay on the bank with Holly, inspecting it in the jam jar while her shoes dried in the sunshine. She opened her journal to check what she had to look for. She could tick quite a few boxes already.

River Water

Clean ☑
Clear ☑
Cool ☑
Not smelly ☑

What else could she find? The lawnmower was further away now and instead she could hear quieter buzzing, whizzing and humming sounds coming from the riverbank.

"Let's go looking for insects, Holly," Tiger said, and off they went.

A glimmering dragonfly hovered above

the reeds before zooming away, and
there was much more to see once Tiger
looked closely. Lying still on her tummy,
a grasshopper bounced right on to her
journal page. Holly leapt into the air as a
small blue butterfly wafted past.

"Well done, Holly," Tiger said. "Just what we were looking for."

River Insects

Dragonflies ☑

Bees ☐

Small blue butterflies ☑

White butterflies ☐

Red admiral butterflies ☐

Grasshoppers ☑

Ladybirds ☐

Tiger turned a page. "Now we'll look for birds, but no chasing them, Holly." She flattened some reeds and made a kind of nest for her and Holly to watch from.

Splash! A duck just like the one she had seen before landed on the river. And then four more came flying in, skiing across the surface before waggling their tails as they folded their wings.

Another bird with a red beak and enormous feet rummaged among the reeds nearby. Tiger didn't know what it was. She drew it so she could ask May Days later.

Something plopped into the water, but Tiger didn't see what it was. She crawled to the edge and looked over the side, her head upside down.

In the mud bank were holes. Tiger checked the list of river mammals she should look out for. There was one thing that the vet hoped Tiger wouldn't find in the river – another otter. Otters needed to live alone. Tiger knew that otters dug dens in riverbanks. This was not a good sign. Tiger went back to the slipway and put on her dry shoes.

"May Days!" she called, running up to the house in a panic. If another otter lived there, it would mean the end of her project and no home for Lucky.

Tiger sat at the kitchen table with her

grandmother and shared the news.

"Let's have a think about this," said May Days. "What size were the holes?"

Tiger made a circle with a finger and thumb, about the size of a ping-pong ball. "This small."

"What size would you say an otter's head is?" said May Days.

Tiger made a bigger circle with two hands, about the size of a tennis ball. "This big."

"Would the otter fit in the hole?"

"No," Tiger said, with relief. May Days gave her some suggestions as to what it might have been, and Tiger made notes in her journal.

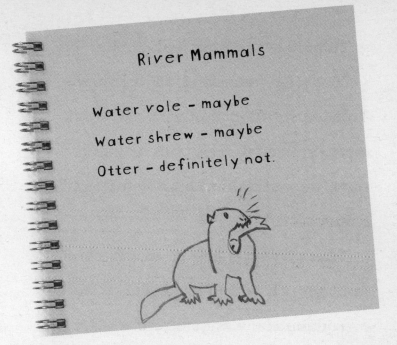

River Mammals

Water vole - maybe
Water shrew - maybe
Otter - definitely not.

"What kind of bird is this?" said Tiger, showing her grandmother a drawing.

"That's a very good drawing!" said May Days. "Looks like a moorhen to me."

Tiger grinned and made another tick on her list.

"What's left to find?" asked May Days.

"A coot, a heron and a kingfisher," said Tiger, and turned another page. "Also some fish, and to make sure there are good, strong muddy banks for otters to make a den."

Tiger would be able to spot the birds from her den or on the riverbank. But everything else was going to be more difficult to find unless she was on the water in a boat...

Chapter 5

Walking the Plank

Tiger was at the boathouse, upstairs in her nature spotter's den, and Tom was downstairs in his pirate den. Tiger was drawing on her map. She coloured the reed bed in green along the edge of the bank by the slipway. She drew tiny bees, butterflies and birds where she had seen them. She was also wondering how to solve the problem of finding fish and strong mud banks without going out on the boat.

Downstairs, Tiger could hear Tom talking to himself. She leaned over the balcony and saw he had a piece of rope in his hands. "Make a hole… the rabbit comes out of the hole… goes round the tree… and back down the hole."

Was Tom doing a wildlife project too? "What are you doing, Tom?"

Tom told her he was practising making a bowline knot. Grumps had taught him a rhyme about a rabbit as a way to remember.

"And that's going to be my treasure chest," Tom said, pointing to a see-through plastic box.

"It needs some decoration," Tiger said.

"I know," said Tom. "But I'm not very
good at that." He was very interested to
see what Tiger was doing too and went
up to her den.

"I wish I had one of those," said Tom, seeing Tiger's map. "It looks like a pirate treasure map."

"It is, sort of," she said, suddenly wondering if the pirate and the nature spotter might be able to join together. And then she had an idea. "I know how we could help each other!"

Tiger would make Tom a treasure map, and Tom would look out for fish and strong muddy banks while he was out sailing. At last they would be a team again.

Later, in the afternoon sunshine, Tom and Grumps set off together in *Spinaway*

with Tom's plastic treasure chest. May
Days joined Tiger on a picnic blanket
along the river's edge where Holly also
sprawled, tummy up. Tiger waved a
fishing net through the water, checking
every now and again to see what was
caught in it. There were plenty of weeds.
Some were long and flat, some were
curly and tangled. Tiger drew them in

her journal before May Days suggested
they go for a walk to see what else they
could spot.

"We need to look out for more birds,"
said Tiger.

The riverbank curved and swerved.
Tiger and her grandmother stepped
through grasses and brambles, willows

and wildflowers, where a white-beaked coot clucked and called out, startled by them coming close. It was quiet enough to hear the grass snap underfoot.

They crouched and parted the reeds. Across on the other bank, standing tall and still as a statue, was a long, thin grey bird called a heron.

River Birds

Duck

Coot

Moorhen

Heron

Kingfisher

All the birds were ticked now, except for the kingfisher. On the other bank, a herd of soft-eyed cows were grazing. Snorty breath puffed from their damp noses as they waded into the edge of the river, interested to see who was over the other side.

"Hello, cows," said Tiger as they swished their tails. "It's just us having a look for a good home for an otter, but you're not on my list."

"Look who else is coming," said May Days a little further along the bank when she saw *Spinaway* heading their way.

"Over here!" called Tiger, waving.

Tom waved back as Grumps dropped the sail and the boat coasted to the bank.

Tom looked excited. "There are loads of muddy places along the bank where the otter could make a holt," he said, which Tiger had explained to him was what an otter's home was called. "And I also found what you most wanted." But it wasn't

diamonds or pearls or gold in his plastic treasure chest.

Tom walked steadily to the bow of the rocking boat, while carrying his chest, which was full of water. He had good sea-legs and didn't spill a drop as he stepped ashore.

In the box, little fish darted about and all sorts of tiny creatures wriggled and squirmed, all of which were good signs that there would be plenty of food for an otter.

"Treasure!" said Tiger and Tom together.

Tiger was releasing all the creatures back into the river when she saw something. She shaded her eyes to see what it was.

A dazzling little bird with a waistcoat

of gold and a cloak of glimmering blue
swooped low over the middle of the water.
It scooped its beak along the water before
flying up and landing further down on a
bare branch sticking out over the river. It
had been fishing.

"It must be a kingfisher!" Tiger
whooped, hoping that May Days would
be surprised that she had guessed what
it was. But once again her grandmother
gently smiled and nodded, and didn't
seem at all surprised that Tiger knew.
Tiger sighed, and decided there and then
that she would give up trying to surprise
May Days.

They all went and sat on the picnic

blanket and shared cloudy lemonade
under a clear sky, amidst the chirp of the
crickets and the whiney zing of gnats.
As they sat there, Tiger went through the
list of fish and the pirates confirmed they
had seen most of them.

The list was complete except for one thing.

"What does an eel look like?" said Tom.

"It looks like a snake," said Tiger. She'd

looked up all the fish that morning in one of May Days's nature books and drawn pictures in her journal. "It's an otter's favourite food."

"Over there on the inside bend where the water is calm might be a good place to find them," said Grumps, pointing to the opposite side of the river. "Why don't we go and have a look? We'll need a nature spotter to identify it, though."

Tiger breathed deeply and thought of how important it was for her to find a home for Lucky the otter. She looked at May Days, whose eyes were wide and blinking. May Days squeezed Tiger's hand, knowing that she was afraid to go on the boat. Tiger was determined to do it, because it would be helping Lucky.

"OK, sail me over," she said. "I'm the nature spotter and I know what eels look like."

Tiger wore a lifejacket and clung tightly to the side of the boat as Grumps pushed away from the bank. Tiger looked up as the sail billowed like a square cloud above her and felt how smoothly and expertly Tom sailed her across. It wasn't as wobbly or scary as she had remembered.

At the bend in the river, Tom tied the rope to a branch of a huge old willow tree that had fallen, the thick trunk leaning out almost horizontally over the water towards the middle.

"I'm going to walk the plank," said Tom, and Grumps gave him a leg up to climb along the fallen tree. The trunk was too curved to walk safely along it, so he sat down, a leg either side, and shuffled along as far as he could.

From the boat and the tree, Tiger and Tom leaned out over the river.

"There!" said Tom, pointing. "Is it an eel?"

"No," said Tiger. "It's a weed." Tiger concentrated hard, as she so wanted to find this last special thing on the list for the otter. In the crystal clear water, she saw a shoal of tiny little greenish fish, each smaller than her smallest finger. She told Tom to be really quiet and stay still

and just keep looking. And then, all of a
sudden, Tiger shouted, "I can see an eel!
I can see two! I can see lots!"

"My goodness!" called May Days who
had heard Tiger from the other bank. "I
wasn't expecting that!"

Tiger stopped clinging to the side of
the boat and stood up, raising her arms,

finding her balance with her feet as the
boat rocked slightly.

"I knew we'd find them, May Days,"
she called across the water. She was
happy May Days *finally* looked surprised,
even if it was because of the eels, rather
than something she'd done. Tiger didn't
feel disappointed as she was too excited

to have found everything on the list
needed for Lucky's new home.

"We did it, Tom!" Tiger beamed at her
friend.

It hadn't been the same without Tom.
But, even though they'd been interested in
their own things, they had found a way to
work together and stay the best of friends.

"I think we are both explorers," Tom said.

"And treasure hunters!" Tiger grinned.

"What did she say? What did she say?"
said Tiger when May Days climbed
into the tent that evening after having
telephoned Miss Popescu. The vet had

been very pleased to hear the good news and would be coming tomorrow.

May Days gave Tiger a big hug. "I'm so proud of how much you cared about finding the otter a good home. And it really surprised me how brave you were when you decided to go out on the boat even though you were scared."

"Did I *really* surprise you?" Tiger asked, a little puzzled. She hadn't even known she was surprising her grandmother when she'd done it. "I thought you were just amazed that there were eels in the river."

"No, it was you who amazed me! And it was marvellous how you and Tom started off not being able to agree, but you have ended up just as good friends as ever."

They laughed to the chirp of the cricket chorus outside as May Days turned out the lamp in the tent.

Tiger was saving some pages in her journal for making more notes about the otter. In the meantime, by the light of a

torch under the covers, she wrote across a
whole page:

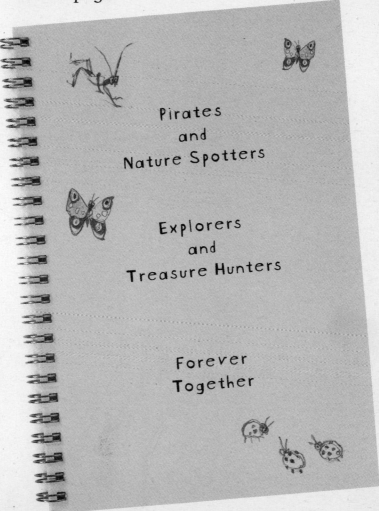

Pirates
and
Nature Spotters

Explorers
and
Treasure Hunters

Forever
Together

Chapter 6

Happy Day

Miss Popescu arrived early with some friends to build a large wire pen for the otter down by the riverbank as his temporary home. There was a stiff-sided paddling pool filled with river water inside the pen, and a wooden box.

"Is it… is it…?" Tiger said, hardly able to catch her breath.

"Yes, a very lucky otter is inside the box," said May Days.

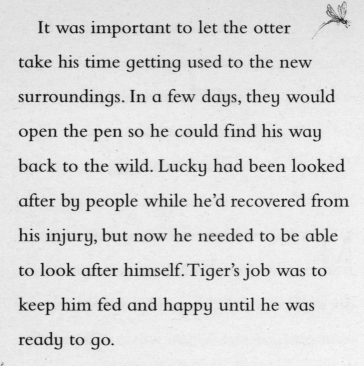

It was important to let the otter take his time getting used to the new surroundings. In a few days, they would open the pen so he could find his way back to the wild. Lucky had been looked after by people while he'd recovered from his injury, but now he needed to be able to look after himself. Tiger's job was to keep him fed and happy until he was ready to go.

Tiger and May Days sat on the pontoon that jutted out over the river, where they could see along the bank to the pen and wooden box in the distance. Sometimes the straw inside shuffled, and sometimes a nose and whiskers wriggled

out and then disappeared again. When
two webbed paws reached out from the
straw, followed by two bright eyes in a
soft brown face, Tiger and May Days
squeezed each other's hands.

"It's so rare to see otters," whispered
May Days.

"He is so beautiful," murmured
Tiger, feeling proud of herself for being
determined to overcome things that
scared and worried her.

May Days had planted flowers in the pots
outside the conservatory. The weather
was glorious. The sun shone with hardly

a cloud in the sky, and warm soft breezes blew along the river. Tom and Grumps went off sailing every day.

Although Tiger and Tom had very different projects, they looked for ways to help each other too. Tom reported on anything new he saw on the river, which Tiger added to her nature spotter's map. Tom collected interesting objects to show everyone, although his treasure chest had now gone missing. He found pale driftwood like bones, pebbles crusty with crystals, and things Tom called leaf skeletons (quite piratey), which were leaves that had crumbled until there was nothing left but the veins. Tiger made a copy of her map for Tom and coloured it in and added all the things he collected, so they both had their own different records.

Tiger wanted to go and watch the otter, but he wouldn't come out if he knew she was there. So she brought one of the big window boards from the

boathouse to hide behind, and propped
it up in front of a large rock in the grass
nearby.

Holly the cat was very interested in
Lucky's bowl of fish and always went
with Tiger to check on the otter. Tiger
had been putting the bowl through a flap
in the pen. It was important not to put her
hands inside if Lucky was out of his box.
Otters had sharp teeth and might mistake
a finger for a small wriggling fish. Tiger
knew Lucky was eating the fish, as it kept
disappearing, but she hadn't seen

him come out of his box since she was with May Days a few days ago.

Miss Popescu called at Willowgate again on her way to work and Tiger read her the report she had made in her journal.

Lucky's progress

Lucky sniffs the air when I bring the fish, but doesn't come out of the box. Fish gone later so he must have eaten it. Saw his nose and whiskers twice. Saw his webbed feet for about three seconds. He doesn't make any sounds.

"Is he happy?" Tiger asked Miss Popsecu. She desperately wanted to see the otter, but was more worried that he was staying in his box because something was wrong.

"Otters are normally playful and inquisitive, but they are shy," said Miss Popescu.

Tiger thought about this. Grumps and Tom loved sailing. May Days and Tiger loved finding wildlife. They were *all* happy doing what they were good at. Tiger had an idea and explained it to Miss Popescu to make sure it was the right thing to do. The vet agreed it would make Lucky happy if he was doing what he was good at too.

Tiger asked Tom to come and help, closely followed by Holly, who smelled suspiciously fishy. Holly had taken some of Lucky's dinner while Tiger put the bowl down and wasn't looking.

"Is it a job for a pirate or a nature spotter?" said Tom.

"Neither," said Tiger, "but it's the kind

of thing we would be good at working out together."

Tiger's idea was to put fish in Lucky's paddling pool so he could feel like he was catching a real fish in the river. The only problem was that the children were not allowed to go in the pen, and they couldn't reach it from outside.

"So how can we get the fish in the paddling pool without him seeing us?" Tiger asked.

"We could throw them over the top of the pen," suggested Tom. "That way it would sound like fish leaping to catch flies and plopping back in the water." Tiger thought this was an excellent idea

and hoped it would encourage Lucky to
come out. They took the bowl of fish to
their hiding place behind the board.

"You throw them and I'll hold the bowl
away from Holly," said Tiger, "otherwise
she'll eat all of Lucky's dinner." With the
fish out of her reach, Holly sauntered off,
nose in the air.

Tom had a good throwing arm. *Splash!*
The piece of fish landed in the pool.
Immediately they heard the straw in the
box shuffling. Tiger peeped over the top
of the board. Lying on his back, the otter
peered over at the pool. His eyes twinkled
brightly.

"Throw another piece," whispered Tiger.

Plop!

Lucky slid out a little way from under the straw. He turned his head on the side, his front webbed paws dangling over his tummy. He wriggled out a little bit more, lay his head back and twitched his nose

and shuffled his shoulders.

"One more," whispered Tiger again.

Splat!

Lucky scampered out of the box. He

looked around to see if anyone was

there, his nose twitching in the air, before

running across to the pool. He circled it
before standing on his hind legs to look
inside. Tiger had to put her hand over her
mouth to stop herself from giggling out
loud as Lucky climbed over the side of the
paddling pool and dived into the water.

Tiger and Tom crouched down against
the board, trying not to laugh as they
heard the water in the pool sloshing
around. And then it all went quiet.

The children peeped over the top
of the board, but there was no sign of
the otter. Perhaps he was swimming
underwater or had gone back in his box?
And then Tiger saw a bright pair of dark
eyes looking up at her. She gasped and

then slowly lowered
herself back down,
pulling Tom with her.

"He's right in front
of us, standing on his
back legs against the
pen," whispered
Tiger.

She and Tom
sat very still, holding their breath.

"I think he can smell the fish," said
Tiger very quietly.

"Shall I throw some more?" said Tom.

"Let's do it all at once and then run
away," said Tiger, knowing that the otter
had to stop relying on people to feed him.

Tiger and Tom grabbed handfuls of fish and together threw them all at once over the top of the pen. They landed in the pool.

Plop! Plop-plop-plop!

The children ran away, but Tiger couldn't help turning back to see Lucky as he dived over the side of the pool and lay on his back happily munching fish with his bright white teeth, as if he had caught them himself.

Tiger and May Days had fish pie for tea while Holly wound around and around their legs.

"This isn't Lucky's dinner, is it?" said Tiger.

"No," said May Days, picking up Holly, who had just jumped up on the table, and putting her back on the floor. "And it's not Holly's either!"

Tiger wrote in her journal.

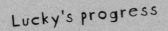

Lucky's progress

Runs around. Dives. Swims in tumbles and turns. Loves eating fish on his back in the pool. Chatters and squeaks when Holly walks past. Not sure if he's saying hello or telling her to stop eating his dinner. He looks happy.

Chapter 7

Letting Go

The next time Miss Popescu came to visit, Tiger told her how Lucky was getting more and more confident in his surroundings and how happy he was. It was time for the next stage of releasing the otter back into the wild where he belonged, and they went down to the pen to prepare, calling for Tom on the way.

"I think Lucky's going to love living on the river," said Tiger.

Tom tied a bowline knot in a long
piece of rope around the latch on the
gate of the pen. Once opened, Lucky was
free to leave when he wanted. Until then,
Tiger would still need to feed him.

"One day you'll come down to the
pen and he'll be gone," said Miss Popescu.
"But then you will have done a great
thing by letting him go."

Hiding behind the board, Tom and
Tiger held the rope and pulled. The latch
popped up and the gate opened.

Lucky didn't leave.

Tiger had been at Willowgate now for

nearly two weeks, but only had two more days left there before she went home.

For three days after the vet's visit and the opening of the gate, Lucky was still eating the fish that Tom and Tiger threw in the pool. He was still diving in his pool, running across the grass and sometimes standing up at the fence. He didn't seem ready to go.

Tiger was in the boathouse working on the pirate map of the river for Tom. She wanted to do something to surprise him for helping her find the eels and all the other important things. When she finished drawing, she managed to find a moment to talk to Grumps by himself as Tom was

busy practising a new rope knot. Then
Tiger asked Tom to come and watch
Lucky with her while Grumps went for a
little sail up the river for Tiger, taking the
pirate map with him…

"This is for you," said Tiger to Tom the
next day, handing over a scroll tied with
a ribbon and sealed with candle wax. It
was the finished pirate map, but when
Tom unravelled it he saw it was actually
a treasure map, with a big X marking the
spot where he could find his prize! Tom
was excited and wanted to hunt for the
treasure right away.

"Please would *everyone* come out in *Spinaway*?" he said. "It's much better when we do things together."

May Days looked unsure. "I've got a few things to do in the… err… conservatory," she said.

"You've already cleaned it," said Tiger, wrinkling her eyebrows together, as she was confused by May Days's answer.

"Oh, but I haven't finished washing the windows," said May Days, and off she went before Tiger could remind her the windows were already sparkling – she had helped her clean them a few days ago!

"Are you coming, Tiger? I'm much better at sailing now," said Tom. "It gets easier when you keep practising things."

Perhaps Tom was right and it would be even easier for Tiger to go on the water this time, so she agreed, feeling only half as scared as last time. Grumps strapped her into a lifejacket and helped her into the boat.

A soft breeze wafted the boat steadily up the river. Tiger relaxed and soon she saw sticklebacks swimming alongside them in the clear water. She heard mayflies fizzing past her ears and smelled the sweet wildflowers on the

banks. Ahead, a trout burst up through the surface to catch a hovering fly and plopped back into the water. *Spinaway* hardly made a sound as it criss-crossed the river. Grumps and Tom sat at the back like captains, their faces turned to the sun, and Tiger felt safe and sound, wondering why she had been so worried before.

Tom steered a course to the spot
marked X on his map, where Tiger had
asked Grumps to bury something for him.
Tom coasted *Spinaway* to the shingle bank
of a small island in the middle of the river
that Tiger had spotted when she'd first
explored the riverbank. They landed with
a gentle bump as Tom lowered the sail.

Tom pulled up some branches and
dug away at the earth with a spade,
while Tiger waited for him to find his
surprise. Buried in the middle under the
trailing branches of a willow tree was his
treasure-chest box. Tiger had decorated it
with brightly coloured buttons and paint,
as if it was made of gold and rubies and

sapphires and emeralds. Burying it in the
earth had made it look old and piratey.
It was the perfect chest for keeping his
river treasure in.

"Open it!" said Tiger, grinning.

"I always wanted one of these!" said Tom, holding up to his eye the telescope that he found inside. Tiger had made it from the cardboard tubes inside the paper towels that she had used to help May Days clean windows.

Pirate Tom was sailing *Spinaway* back home, looking through his telescope now and again while they coasted on the current, when all of a sudden Tiger saw something unexpected. She gasped, not because she felt worried, but because it was something wonderful.

"Tom," she whispered. "Stop here!"

Without asking why, Tom lowered

the anchor over the side of the boat and dropped the sail, so they could float where they were.

Grumps leaned in, whispering, as it seemed the right thing to do. "What's going on?"

Tiger couldn't believe her eyes. Lucky was on the concrete slipway slope. He was ready to leave and find a new home. Everyone held their breath and stayed still and watched.

Lucky turned round and was about to head back along the bank to his pen, but then stopped as if he had changed his mind. Instead he went to the end of the

pontoon and leaned over the edge, his head waving around. He looked down at the water, holding on with his claws and webbed feet.

"Sometimes you have to let go," Tiger whispered. The most important thing would be for him to decide to go by himself.

And Lucky did. Bubbles burst to the surface where he dived, and he disappeared into his new home.

Tiger cuddled Holly in bed that night, thinking of Lucky's arched back as he'd swum away through the water, ready to find his own home in the wild. He didn't come back for his dinner and wouldn't come back again.

"Do you think we'll ever see Lucky again?" she whispered to her grandmother in the dark.

"Would you mind if we didn't?" asked May Days.

Tiger smiled to herself. "No, because he's happy."

Chapter 8

Diamonds

On the last day of the holiday, Tiger was feeling more confident about going sailing with the pirates. She wanted one more trip on the river with everyone before her dad returned to take her home later that day.

Once again, May Days was about to wave them all off from the pontoon, saying she had things to do. "I must finish mowing the lawn," she said. "Have fun!"

"But you finished the mowing," said
Tiger.

"Oh," she said, and it surprised Tiger to
see May Days looking flustered. "Actually,
I was going to plant up the pots."

"They are already full of flowers!" said
Tiger. Something was definitely up.

And then Tiger worked it out... May
Days was about to make another excuse,
but Tiger went over and hugged her.

"Are you afraid of going on the water
too?" she whispered.

It wasn't that May Days didn't like to
sail. She was afraid of falling in as she
hadn't learned to swim very well when
she was young.

"I'm rather embarrassed and feel a bit silly when all of you are so brave," she said.

"This will be the third time I've been in the boat and I'm only a quarter as scared now compared to the first time," said Tiger to reassure her grandmother.

"Thank you, that makes me feel much better," said May Days.

"You could have swimming lessons," Tiger suggested. "But please come, just this once. If I can do it, you can too."

"We wear lifejackets on board," said Tom. "You won't sink if you are wearing one of these."

"Everyone has something they are afraid of," said Tiger to May Days.

"But you can hold on to me."

"I feel braver already," her

grandmother said. Grumps and Tom

helped her down into the boat. "Oh my," she added, "I am feeling rather wobbly."

May Days and Tiger held hands, and also held a side of the boat each, as Tom steered the tiller and lowered or raised the sail to catch the breeze.

They sailed to where the cows came down to the river to gaze at them with soft brown eyes.

Then they sailed back home as the setting sun reflected on the water and made the river turn pink and orange.

"What is the most treasured thing you have found this holiday?" May Days asked everyone.

"Gold," said Tom, digging into his

pocket and bringing out a stone.

"Gold?" said Tiger. Where had he found such treasure?

Tom showed them a stone he had found with a golden line running through it. "Actually, I looked it up in a book and it's not real gold. But I wish it was so I could sell it and have enough money to buy another boat because I want to race Grumps and see who is the fastest pirate on the seas!"

Grumps ruffled Tom's hair. "Maybe one day," he laughed.

"What is the most treasured thing you have found this holiday, Tiger?" asked May Days.

Tiger had seen so much wildlife, all of
it wonderful, all of it treasured. Just then,
the water rippled under the surface. Tiger
put a finger to her lips to tell everybody
to be quiet and look where she pointed.
"There's my best treasure."

Only metres from the boat was Lucky,
swimming through the water. Bubbles of
air, caught in his waterproof fur, made
him look as if he was coated in diamonds.

He surfaced and his nose twitched and
his whiskers curled as he blinked at the
four people in the boat, their eyes bright,
their smiles beaming.

"Dad, have you ever been sailing in a
proper boat?" said Tiger after she'd blown
a hundred kisses to May Days and Holly
and Tom and Grumps from the window
of the car as they'd driven away from
Willowgate House.

"No, I get scared on the water because
I don't like falling in. Remember that
time at the seaside when we had a
blow-up boat?"

"I was thinking about that the other day," said Tiger, smiling. "Maybe you should come sailing with me and my friend Tom. He will make you feel so much better about it."

"Did you find an opportunity to surprise May Days?" asked her dad.

"Yes."

"How did you do that?" he said, knowing how hard it was to surprise his mother.

"Because anyone can be surprising when you don't expect them to be."

Would it ever again be as good a holiday as this time at Willowgate? Tiger would have to wait and see.

SARAH LEAN

A shy cat
who wants to
make friends...

The
Secret
Cat

Meet Tiger Days – the little girl who loves to help animals.

Tiger's grandmother looks after animals
in need, and when Tiger comes to stay she
quickly learns how to feed a baby warthog
and keep it safe.

Tiger already has her hands full when a
mysterious sound leads her to another
little animal…

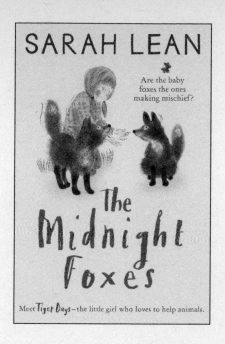

Are the baby foxes the ones making mischief?

SARAH LEAN

The Midnight Foxes

Meet Tiger Days – the little girl who loves to help animals.

This time at Willowgate House Tiger discovers a mysterious tunnel that has appeared under the shed and someone – or something – has been burying eggs in the garden...

Tiger and her friend Tom decide to become detectives – determined to crack the case!